The
TORTILLA
FACTORY

The
TORTILLA
FACTORY

Gary Paulsen

PAINTINGS BY

Ruth Wright Paulsen

Voyager Books

Harcourt, Inc.

ORLANDO   AUSTIN   NEW YORK   SAN DIEGO   LONDON

For information about permission to reproduce selections from this book, write to trade.
permissions@hmhco.com or to Permissions, Houghton Mifflin Harcourt Publishing Company,
3 Park Avenue, 19th Floor, New York, New York 10016.

www.hmhco.com

First Voyager books edition 1998
Voyager Books is a registered trademark of Harcourt, Inc.

Library of Congress Cataloging-in-Publication Data
Paulsen, Gary
The tortilla factory / by Gary Paulsen; illustrated by
Ruth Wright Paulsen—1st ed.
p.   cm.
"Voyager Books."
ISBN 978-0-15-292876-6
ISBN 978-0-15-201698-2 pb
1. Tortillas—Juvenile literature. [1. Tortillas.]
I. Paulsen, Ruth Wright, ill. II. Title.
TX770.T65P38   1995
641.8´2—dc20   93-48590

PRINTED IN CHINA

SCP 30 29 28 27 26
4500607747

…Through Your goodness we have this bread to offer,
Which earth has given and human hands have made.
It will become for us the bread of life.

—*The Sacramentary of the Roman Missal*

The black earth sleeps in winter.

But in the spring the black earth
is worked by brown hands

that plant yellow seeds,

which become green plants rustling in soft wind

for the tortilla factory,

where laughing people and clank-clunking
machinery mix the flour into dough,

and push the dough,
and squeeze the dough,
and flatten the dough…

…and bake the dough into perfect disks that
come off the machine and into a package
and onto a truck and into a kitchen

to be wrapped around juicy beans

and eaten by white teeth, to fill a round stomach

and give strength to the brown hands
that work the black earth

to plant yellow seeds,

which make golden corn to be dried
in hot sun and be ground into flour. . . .

The paintings in this book were done in oil on linen.
The display type was set in Deepdene and Greco Deco.
The text type was set in Dante.
Color separations by Bright Arts, Ltd., Singapore
Printed and bound by RR Donnelley, China
Production supervision by Stanley Redfern and Jane Van Gelder
Designed by Michael Farmer